22

STACEY'S Extraordinary WORDS

BY
STACEY ABRAMS

ILLUSTRATED BY
KITT THOMAS

BALZER + BRAY
An Imprint of HarperCollinsPublishers

Balzer + Bray is an imprint of HarperCollins Publishers.

Stacey's Extraordinary Words
Text copyright © 2021 by Stacey Abrams
Illustrations copyright © 2021 by Kitt Thomas
For information address HarperCollins Children's Books,
a division of HarperCollins Publishers, 195 Broadway, New York, NY 10007.
www.harpercollinschildrens.com

ISBN 978-0-06-320947-3 — ISBN 978-0-06-323919-7 (special edition)

The artist used Procreate to create the digital illustrations for this book.
Typography Dana Fritts
Hand lettering by Laura Mock
21 22 23 24 25   PC   10 9 8 7 6 5 4 3 2 1
❖
First Edition

To my first storytellers—Mom and Dad.
To my bibliophile siblings all. And to our newest
generation of readers: Jorden, Faith, Cameron, Riyan,
Ayren, and Devin.

—S.A.

To those I love most: Mom; Dad;
my brother, Desmond; and Garfield—
the little cat who saved my life.
—K.T.

Stacey loved words. She loved to read and write and say them. She adored fun words, long words, unusual words. Words with wonderful histories and weird combinations.

Whenever Stacey learned a new word, it was like making a new friend. First, she would find the dictionary. Then she would look up where the word had come from and learn its secrets. Did any of its letters hide and stay quiet? Like the *p* in *ptarmigan*, a bird that lives in cold, northern regions. Or were they strong like the *i* in *bright*?

Next, she wrote the word in her special Notebook of Extraordinary Words. She practiced how to arrange the letters just right. How to sound them out. That's because she loved spelling interesting words most of all.

O

ON-O-MATO-POE-A

POP

With her favorite words, she would try to remember their quirks—what made them special. When she saw a superlong word like *onomatopoeia*, a funny word to describe the sounds of other words, she had to jump and sway. Words like *duckling* made her grin. *Persnickety* tickled her tongue.

Sometimes Stacey thought that words understood her better than people did. When she sat by herself during recess, they never teased her about being quiet. Or about being clumsy when she fell. Or awkward when the joke in her head came out wrong.

When she read books under the covers, words never told her to go to sleep. Words understood why she was grumpy or anxious. In fact, words helped her explain what she was feeling—if only to herself.

One day, Stacey's teacher, Mrs. Blakeslee, asked her to wait after class. She squirmed in her seat because she was afraid. Petrified (another way to say really, really afraid)! Usually, the teacher only kept a student after class because of a blunder—a mistake.

Mrs. Blakeslee called Stacey to her desk, and she returned her spelling test. A big red 100 sat at the top of the page. The teacher asked her, "Do you know what a spelling bee is?"

"A really smart insect?" Stacey joked.

The teacher smiled. "A spelling bee is a contest where students compete to spell as many words correctly as they can. I would like for you to participate."

Stacey couldn't believe it. "Who else will be there?"

"I am nominating you and Jake. The spelling bee is next week."

Stacey's excitement suddenly evaporated.

Jake was not her friend. He was a bully who knew words too. Just yesterday, he had used a complicated word that made Suki cry. Last week, she heard him say something cruel to Zivko about his accent. Stacey thought it was stupendous that Zivko knew words in two different languages.

Stacey knew as many words as Jake did. She wanted to say something when he said mean things to her friends, but she was intimidated—scared. Because sometimes he said hurtful things to her too.

She wished she had used her clever words to help Suki or Zivko or herself by speaking up.

Perhaps at this spelling bee she would be braver. At the spelling bee, she would not be silent.

All week long, Stacey studied her spelling words from school and the ones she kept in her notebook.

Still, the spelling bee felt as far away as the longest word she had ever seen: sesquipedalian. (A fancy way to describe words with lots of syllables.)

The days of the week were monotonous, torturous, and sluggish—every hour felt longer and longer.

TORTUROUS

MONOTONOUS

SLUGGISH

Stacey wished for the week to whisk its days away.

Finally, the morning of the spelling bee arrived. Stacey walked into the county library with her mother, holding her hand tight.

Momma gave her a big hug and whispered into her ear, "Just do your best. Your dad and I are very proud of you."

Stacey followed her teacher to the room where the other students waited until it was time to go. Then they went onto a stage. The announcer explained the rules.

Kids stepped up to the microphone one by one to get their word. If they spelled it right, the announcer told them so. But if they made a mistake, a bell would ring. The student would have to leave the stage. No do-overs.

Stacey's turn finally came. Her stomach ached with nervous energy. But she was ready.

Say the word. "Dither."

Sound it out. "Di-ther."

Spell it. "D-I-T-H-E-R."

"That is correct."
The announcer called on the next student. And the next.

Promptly. Enormous. Shudder. Transportation. Craggy. Reception. Village.

Finally, only three contestants remained.
Stacey and Jake and a girl from another school.
The girl went up to spell her word. *Ding!* She had spelled *chocolate* without the second *o*.

"We are down to our final two contestants," the announcer told the audience.

Jake took a long time to spell *except*.

Stacey got *squeezed* but she remembered the lost letters she adored, like *q* and *z*.

Jake tackled *clambering*.

EX...

...CE

...PT 20

SQ

UEE

ZED

19

Stacey conquered *disengage*.

Then Jake defeated *geometry*.

Stacey returned to the podium ready to do battle with her next word. She repeated it. She pronounced it. She spelled it. "I-N-S-T-A-N-T-A-N-I-O-U-S. Instantaneous."

As she waited for the announcer, the bell dinged. "I'm sorry, that is incorrect. The proper spelling is . . ."

Stacey couldn't hear the rest of what he said. Tears filled her eyes, but she stayed onstage like a good sport as Jake got his trophy and she received her second-place ribbon. Everyone congratulated Jake and so did she.

"Good job."
Jake laughed and rolled his eyes. "At least
I know the difference between *i* and *e*."

Stacey felt embarrassed, but she refused to let Jake make her cry. "Well, I misspelled my word, but I do know how to be courteous. You should try it."

She turned away and went to find her mom.

If today were like one of the stories Stacey loved most, she would have won. And Jake would have learned that words were a gift that shouldn't be used to hurt people.

But things didn't always happen that way in real life. Sometimes change was harder. And it didn't happen right away.

Stacey felt a hand brush at her cheek. It opened her fist and smoothed out the ribbon. "Momma?"

She put a butterscotch candy on top, Stacey's favorite kind. "You okay?"

"I lost."

"But you came so far. Nearly to the very end."

"Not far enough. I got the letter wrong. And I didn't win. I failed."

"You only fail if you stop," her mother reminded her.
"I know there's a word for that. You know it too."
Stacey thought about one of her favorite words.
"Perseverance. P-E-R-S-E-V-E-R-A-N-C-E."

"Exactly. So let's go home and learn
more words. There's always next year."

Stacey imagined all the words she had yet to
meet—new words and new ways to speak up and
help others. She'd find them all.
"No, Momma. There's always tomorrow."

Author's Note

I love words. I can't remember ever not loving them. As a preschooler, when class ended, my parents were still hard at work. Luckily, I attended preschool on the college campus where my mother served as librarian. She would have us nap in the stacks as she continued to work, and I nestled with books and stories and words. Even today, the rich scent of a library or the waft of a freshly opened book makes me smile.

Not only were words my companions, they were also my protectors. One day during first grade, the principal of Anniston Avenue Elementary fetched me from class and walked me outside to one of the trailers that lined the back of the school building. My next memory is of the door opening wide and a lovely woman greeting me. Mrs. Blakeslee—my soon-to-be second-grade teacher.

Unbeknownst to me, I had been moved up a grade in the middle of the term. As a new kid in class, the strongest, most familiar sight was the books on the shelves near the front of class. My teacher invited me to read as many of them as I wished. In

those uneasy first days, while other kids played at recess, I read quietly, unsure of my place—until I opened the pages of a good story. There, I could hide from the older children who teased me and revel in the victories of others. When Mrs. Blakeslee chose me for the spelling bee that year, her act of kindness nudged me out of the books and into a world I had never imagined.

My first spelling bee combined my greatest joy and biggest fear: talking about words and making mistakes. More than forty years later, these remain the stalwart axes against which I measure my growth. In that contest, I learned in front of a live audience that *chocolate* has two *o*'s. When the bell dinged, I practiced stoicism before I knew of the concept. And I still recall my mom pressing the yellow candy into my hand, remembering that I, her second of six children, loved that color most. Because of that first lost spelling bee, followed by four more close calls until I claimed victory in sixth grade, I discovered how to merge my delight and my terror, realizing that failure is never more than an invitation to try again.

Like Jake, some kids picked on me and others who were different. Over the years, I learned how to use my words to do good, even when I am most afraid. I constantly strive to speak up, especially when it makes me nervous. And if I am doing my very best, I make room for those who haven't discovered their superpowers. Yet.

Stacey's Notebook of Extraordinary Words

- **anxious** (ang·shuhs): filled with worry
- **awkward** (aa·kwurd): lacking in confidence or skill
- **blunder** (bluhn·dur): a mistake
- **bright** (brite): giving off lots of light
- **chocolate** (chaa·kluht): a yummy dessert *Remember the second "o"!*
- **clambering** (klam·bur·eeng): using your hands and feet to climb a difficult path
- **complicated** (kaam·pluh·kay·tuhd): including many parts
- **conquered** (kaan·kurd): took control by force
- **courteous** (kur·tee·uhs): to treat others with kindness and respect
- **craggy** (kra·gee): rough or uneven
- **cruel** (krooel): when someone is mean on purpose
- **defeated** (duh·fee·tuhd): won in a competition *Weirdly, it can also mean losing!*
- **disengage** (di·suhn·gayj): to release or separate from something
- **dither** (di·thur): to be unsure
- **duckling** (duh·kluhng): a baby duck
- **enormous** (uh·nor·muhs): very large

- **evaporated** (uh·va·pur·ay·tuhd): to disappear into the air
- **except** (uhk·sept): not including *Not to be mixed up with accept, where you do receive something!*
- **geometry** (jee·aa·muh·tree): a type of math that measures the surface of shapes
- **grumpy** (gruhm·pee): in a bad mood
- **instantaneous** ✗ ✗ ✗ (in·stuhn·tay·nee·uhs): when something happens immediately *But don't give up if it doesn't. Most things take time and lots of practice!*
- **intimidated** (in·ti·muh·day·tuhd): not confident in yourself
- **monotonous** (muh·naa·tuh·nuhs): when something stays the same
- **onomatopoeia** (aa·nuh·maa·tuh·pee·uh): a word to describe the sounds of other words
- **perseverance** ♡ (pur·suh·vee·ruhns): always willing to try again and never give up *One of my favorite words!*
- **persnickety** (pur·sni·kuh·tee): to be very particular about things
- **petrified** (peh·truh·fide): really, really afraid *It can also mean when something is converted into stone.*

- **promptly** (praampt·lee): when something happens very quickly
- **ptarmigan** (taar·muh·gin): a bird that lives in cold, northern regions *Remember, the "p" is silent!*
- **reception** (ruh·sep·shun): an event where you welcome someone *It can also mean when you receive something—like a reaction*
- **sesquipedalian** (seh·skwuh·puh·day·lee·uhn): a word with lots of syllables
- **shudder** (shuh·dur): to shiver or shake
- **sluggish** (sluh·guhsh): very slow
- **stupendous** (stoo·pen·duhs): another word for amazing
- **squeezed** (skweezd): held too tight *Remember the lost letters like "q" and "z."*
- **tackled** (ta·kuhld): worked hard to deal with a difficult task
- **torturous** (tor·tschur·us): very unpleasant or painful
- **transportation** (tran·spor·tay·shun): a way to get from one place to another
- **village** (vi·luhj): a place smaller than a town, where people live together
- **whisk** (wisk): to move quickly